1: The Secret of Weeping Wood

"Babies!" cried Jillo. "It's babies crying. The story's true. Let's get out of here."

They needed no urging. As the chilling cries grew louder, they fled, pelting through the trees, swerving to avoid collision with the close, thick trunks. They burst sobbing from the haunted thicket and ran on till the cries of the phantom infants faded and they could run no more.

Look out for the Outfit's other adventures:

THE OUTFIT

1: The Secret of Weeping Wood

Robert Swindells

Hippo

Scholastic Children's Books
Commonwealth House, 1–19 New Oxford Street,
London WC1A 1NU, UK
a division of Scholastic Ltd
London ~ New York ~ Toronto ~ Sydney ~ Auckland

First published by Scholastic Ltd, 1993
This edition published by Scholastic Ltd, 1997

Text copyright © Robert Swindells, 1993

ISBN 0 590 19143 8

Typeset by TW Typesetting, Midsomer Norton, Somerset
Printed by Cox & Wyman Ltd, Reading, Berks.

10 9 8 7 6 5

1. No Such Thing

"Badgers?" Jillo's face lit up. "I never knew we had badgers in Weeping Wood."

Mickey nodded. "Oh, yes. A whole family of them. I've seen them lots of times."

"How come I've never seen them, then? After all, it's our wood – Mum's and Dad's, I mean!"

Mickey chuckled. "They're your badgers, come to that, but you never will see 'em if you rush off home at eight o'clock every night."

"I can't help that, Mickey, and you know it. My dad's very strict. If I don't get Titch home by eight at the latest, he goes ape-shape."

"Huh!" Titch scowled at her older sister. "Get Titch home? Titch can get herself home just as easily as you can. I'm not a baby. I'm seven."

Jillo nodded. "I know, but try telling Dad that. He thinks I'm still a baby, and I'm nine. I bet he'll still want me in by eight when I'm a hundred."

"When you're a hundred," laughed Mickey, "your dad will be about a hundred-and-fifty. He won't be chasing you around much."

"Oh, I don't know," said Shaz. "My grandad still chases me around sometimes, and he's very old."

Jillo shook her head. "No, he doesn't, Shaz. You've stayed out all night sometimes. You told me. You're lucky, you and Mickey. My parents never go away and leave Titch and me behind."

Shaz grinned. "Well, they haven't

got dozens of relatives in Pakistan, have they? That's where my parents are – visiting family."

"And they're not dealers, like my dad," said Mickey. "They don't have to be on the road all the time, buying and selling. They've got a farm and a proper house, not a tin one on wheels like this one."

"Well, I still think you're both lucky. You can do more or less as you please most of the time." She looked at Mickey. "The only bit I wouldn't like is not having a mum. That must be sad."

"I've got one," protested Mickey. "She just doesn't live here, that's all."

"Where does she live?" asked Titch.

Mickey shrugged. "Dunno."

"That is sad," murmured Jillo.

Mickey shook his head. "No, it isn't. I'm used to it. Anyway." He looked at them. "Who wants to see badgers tonight?"

3

Shaz raised his hand. "I do."

Mickey gazed at Titch and Jillo. "What about you two? You're members of The Outfit too, and The Outfit sticks together. You took the vow."

"I know we did," said Jillo. "But it's harder for us. What time would we be finished?"

"Oh – let's see. It gets dark about eight o'clock, so the badgers'll be out just after that. I reckon you could get a good look at them and be home for nine. How about that?"

Jillo looked dubious. "An hour late. It'd mean trouble."

"Big trouble?"

"Dunno. Depends what mood Dad's in."

"Take a chance, eh? Just this once?"

Jillo looked at Titch. "What d'you say, Titch? Shall we risk it?"

Titch grinned and nodded.

Jillo sighed. "Okay, Mickey. Count

4

us in. I just hope we don't hear the ghosts, that's all."

"Ghosts?" Mickey smiled, shaking his head. "I've lived in this caravan, in these woods, for as long as I can remember, and I've never heard babies crying. It's a tale, Jillo. I don't believe in ghosts. There's no such thing."

2. Sycamore Thicket

When Jillo and Titch got to the caravan at half-past seven, Shaz was already there, helping Mickey with the washing up. Raider was helping too, licking bacon grease and scraps of rind from a tin plate. Raider was Mickey's dog. He was a lurcher with a wiry grey coat and intelligent eyes. He was Mickey's devoted companion, following him everywhere except when ordered to stay and guard the caravan. Jillo suspected it was Raider who supplied the Wilburys with rabbits for the delicious pies they occasionally ate. He was gentle most of the time, but you wouldn't get past him if he was on guard.

"Hello, Raider," cried Titch, scratching the dog's ears. "Bacon for tea, eh?"

"Lucky hound," growled Jillo. "You too, Mickey. We had rotten old macaroni cheese and salad."

Mickey grinned. "Didn't have to cook it yourself though, did you? Or wash up after."

"I'd cook and wash up if we could have sausages and burgers and hot dogs like you do all the time, but there's no chance. Mum's a healthy eating freak."

"She's there though, isn't she?" said Mickey.

"Oh, yes," said Jillo. "She's always there." Poor old Mickey, she thought. No mum.

"Are we off, then?" Shaz enquired, hanging the tea towel on its hook. Mickey emptied the washing up water into the tiny sink and wiped it round. "Might as well. Be dark soon." He pulled down his shirt sleeves and buttoned them.

"Let's do the oath," suggested Titch. She liked the oath, because she'd helped to make it up.

"Okay," smiled Mickey, who liked it too. They joined hands, squatted in a circle with Raider in the middle and chanted in unison:

"Faithful, fearless, full of fun,
Winter, summer, rain or sun,
One for five and five for one –
THE OUTFIT!"

They shouted the last line and sprang upright, arms raised high.

"Woof!" went Raider, and they broke the circle, laughing.

"Stay," said Mickey to Raider as they piled out of the caravan. "On guard." The dog looked wistful but obeyed, watching from the top of the wooden steps as the four walked off into the twilit wood. Normally they'd have taken him along but tonight they hoped to see badgers, and badgers don't appear when there's a dog about.

Twilight deepened as they followed Mickey through the trees. Somewhere a sleepy blackbird called, but apart from that and their footfalls, the wood was silent. After a while Titch said, "Where we going, Mickey?" She had the shortest legs and it was hard for her to keep up.

"Sycamore Thicket," he told her. "The badgers' set is just near there."

"Oooh!" Titch shivered. "I didn't know we were going there. That's where the ghosts are."

"I told you there's no such thing," said Mickey. "And anyway, if you want to be part of The Outfit you've got to be brave."

"I am brave," protested Titch. "I was just saying, that's all."

They went on. Now it was almost dark. The blackbird had gone to sleep. An owl screeched in the distance, making them jump. Twigs cracked beneath their trainers as they walked. Sycamore Thicket loomed ahead – the densest, darkest part of Weeping Wood. Mickey raised a hand. They stopped.

"Right." Mickey spoke in a whisper. "The set's over there, but we want to get downwind of it or the badgers'll catch our scent and stay underground." He jabbed the air with a finger. "We'll circle this way. Stay behind me, and be as quiet as you can."

He moved off and they followed, creeping between the close-crowded trunks of the thicket. Little sunlight penetrated here even in midsummer, and there was no undergrowth – just a thick, moist carpet of fallen leaves. A rank smell rose from this carpet as the four children tiptoed stealthily across it. Presently Mickey raised his hand again and they stopped, huddling together in the chill gloom.

"Okay." Mickey pointed, whispering. "It's over there, see? In the side of that mound. Got it?" They nodded. "Right. Now we wait. No talking."

They waited, straining their eyes. Nothing stirred near the dark mound. Jillo glanced at her watch. Five to eight. Dad would expect to see Titch and her at any moment now. She pushed the thought aside, gazing at the mound. Was that – was there a bit of white moving in the mouth of the set? There seemed to be, but she wasn't sure. Your eyes start playing tricks when you stare into the dark. She'd just decided she was mistaken when

Mickey hissed, "There, see?"

It was a beautiful badger. Only the white bits showed clearly, but if you screwed up your eyes you could see its sleek shape against the black shadow of the mound. After a moment the creature was joined by a second badger, and as the children watched, the pair began ambling away from the set, snuffling the leaf-carpet as they came. They were actually coming towards the children. Jillo saw bright eyes, moist snouts. How close would they come, she wondered, before they detected the presence of humans and fled? Mickey, raised in the woods, had chosen their vantage point well, and the creatures were no more than eight metres away when the noise began.

"What's that?" Titch grabbed her sister's arm as the plaintive sound rose on the breeze. The badgers had whirled and were scuttling with surprising speed towards the safety of their set.

Shaz looked at Mickey. "It sounds like – like –"

"Babies!" cried Jillo. "It's babies crying. The story's true. Let's get out of here."

They needed no urging. As the chilling cries grew louder, they fled, pelting through the trees, swerving to avoid collision with the close, thick trunks. They burst sobbing from the haunted thicket and ran on till the cries of the phantom infants faded and they could run no more.

3. Scared, or What?

"Morning, Jillo." Shaz grinned. "Did you get into trouble last night?"

Jillo shook her head. "We were in by a quarter-past eight. Dad said something weird, though."

"What?"

"He said, 'What's the matter with you two – you look as though you've seen a ghost.'"

"He didn't."

"He did."

"What did you say?"

"What could I say? I laughed and told him we saw a badger."

It was Friday morning. Jillo, Titch and Shaz were in the school playground. There was no sign of Mickey, but that wasn't unusual. When his dad was away, Mickey had to get himself up in the morning, and he wasn't very good at it. He was often late for school, and sometimes he didn't show up at all. He was always in trouble with the teachers, but he didn't seem to care.

"Well," smiled Shaz, "you didn't see a ghost and you did see a badger, so you told the truth."

"But not the whole truth," said Titch. "We didn't say we heard a ghost."

Jillo looked at her sister. "It would have been a waste of breath, Titch. He'd have laughed at us."

"But it's true though, isn't it?" said Shaz. "We did hear babies crying, just as the old story says."

Jillo shivered, remembering. "Yes. It

seems impossible now, in broad daylight – as though we dreamed it or
something, but we didn't."

"I want to hear them again," said
Titch.

Jillo looked at her. "Are you crazy?
I'm never going anywhere near
Sycamore Thicket again as long as I
live."

Titch chuckled. "Scared, or what?"

"I'm not scared, so there. I just don't
feel like going there again, that's all."

"Hello, everybody." Mickey appeared, grinning as usual. His hair was
sticking out all over the place. He
looked at Jillo. "Going where again?"

"Sycamore Thicket."

"Oh, but we've got to go again. I
mean, we're The Outfit, right? Fearless, it says in the oath. We've proved
that babies do cry in Weeping Wood –
now we've got to find out why."

"*You've* got to find out why!" cried

Jillo. "Not me. I don't care why."

"I do!" piped Titch. "I'll come with you, Mickey."

"Me too," said Shaz. They all looked at Jillo.

"Aw – come on," urged Mickey. "For the sake of The Outfit."

Jillo bit her lip. "When?"

Mickey shrugged. "Tonight, if you like. It's Saturday tomorrow – no school. Maybe your dad'll let you stay out a bit later."

"Perhaps he will," murmured Jillo. "But I'm not sure I want to."

"It's not fair," said Titch. "If you don't come, Dad won't let me out at all."

"Yeah," growled Shaz.

"Not fair," muttered Mickey.

"Oh, all right," said Jillo. "I'll come, on one condition."

"What's that?" asked Mickey.

"That we take Raider along."

He nodded. "Okay. Half-seven at my place?"

"Half-seven," said Shaz. "I'll bring my cassette recorder."

"What on earth for?" asked Mickey.

"To record the crying."

Jillo smiled wryly. "Which crying?" she asked. "Mine, or the ghosts'?"

4. Mickey Gets it Wrong

It seemed a long day at school. The four friends might have discussed the mystery in whispers when the teacher wasn't looking, but they were all in different classes so they couldn't. They could think about it though, and that's what they did, and so none of them managed to learn very much from their lessons.

Mickey's class was doing the Romans. It was an interesting topic and Mickey usually enjoyed it. He and two class-mates were building a model ballista – a war engine the Romans used to hurl great stones at their enemies. The model was made of balsa wood, and it was nearly ready for painting. Other kids were building an aqueduct, a fort, a galley and a villa. Ten children were working on the villa. Halfway through the period, Mrs Latimer stopped the work and had four of them carry the model to her table. It was built on a big square of chipboard. The teacher stood behind it and spoke to the class.

"This model is unfinished," she said, "but I want us to look at a certain part of it now, because this part will be covered up when the villa is complete. Gather round, please."

The children gathered round Mrs Latimer's table. There was some pushing and shoving, which the teacher stopped by frowning at the culprits over her half-moon spectacles. "Now." She pointed to the floor in one of the villa's rooms. "This floor," she said, "will be covered with a decorative mosaic. Gillian – what's a mosaic?"

"Please Miss, it's a pattern or picture made from tiny pieces of marble and coloured stone."

Mrs Latimer nodded. "That's right. All of the floors in this villa will have mosaics, but it's what lies beneath these floors that I want us to look at now. Darren – what do you see?"

"Miss – a sort of space, Miss."

"That's right, Darren. A sort of space. What else?" Several children raised their hands. "Kylie?" "Miss, there's like pillars, holding up the floor."

Mrs Latimer smiled. "Excellent. Now, can anybody remember what this space is for. We talked about it two weeks ago. Yes, Liam?"

"Please Miss, it's for central heating. They had fires under the villa to fill the space with hot air. It warmed the rooms, Miss."

"That's right, Liam. Think of it."

Mrs Latimer's eyes shone. "Central heating, two thousand years ago. And that's only one of hundreds of clever devices invented by the Romans." She looked at the class. "Can anybody remember what the Romans called this device?"

"Hypo – something, Miss," volunteered Kylie.

Mrs Latimer smiled. "Hypocaust," she said. "Back to work now, everybody."

Mickey joined his group round the ballista, but he couldn't concentrate. He kept thinking about tonight. He'd put on a brave face for the others, but he didn't really fancy Sycamore Thicket. Not now. Like most people in Lenton, he'd always considered the story about phantom babies a tale – a local legend with no shred of truth in it. Now he'd actually heard their cries, and that changed everything.

Still, he mused, we're The Outfit, aren't we? We've spent the best part of a year looking for a real adventure, and now we've found one. Can't just leave it, can we? Can't go crying to the grown-ups either – who'd believe us? Mind you – he smiled to himself, if the babies cry tonight, and Shaz gets them on his cassette recorder, we'll have –

"Michael Wilbury!"

"Er – yes, Miss?" Mickey's brain reeled. He'd been caught dreaming.

"Name one clever invention of the Romans."

"Miss – er – er – the cassette recorder, Miss."

5. Will o' the Wisp

"What's that you're writing, Mickey?" The caravan's door was open as usual, so Jillo had walked right in with Titch at her heels.

Mickey, at the table, covered the sheet of paper with his arms. "It's nothing."

"It can't be nothing. Come on – what is it? Letter to your dad?"

"Huh!" Mickey shook his head. "Fat lot of use that'd be – Dad can only read his name. It's lines, if you must know."

"Lines? How many? Who for? What did you do?"

"A hundred," said Mickey, gloomily.

"For Mrs Latimer. I must not be cheeky."

"Why?" Titch's eyes twinkled. "What did you say to her?"

"I said the cassette recorder was a Roman invention, but I didn't mean to. She took me by surprise."

"And how many have you done?" asked Jillo.

"Sixty."

"Aw heck – so we've got to hang around while you do forty more?"

" 'Fraid so. Anyway, Shaz isn't here yet."

Mickey wrote on. Jillo and Titch went outside and threw sticks for Raider to fetch till they saw Shaz coming through the trees.

"Better late than never," said Jillo. Shaz pulled a face.

"Sorry if I've kept everybody waiting, 'cause I've only come to say I can't stay."

"Can't stay? Why not?"

Shaz shrugged. "My grandad. He's in a funny mood. Says I go out too much. I've got to stay in tonight and help him clean the house."

"How boring. Can't you tell him to go take a running jump at himself?"

Shaz gazed at her. "Could you tell your dad that?"

"You're joking!"

"Well, then." He stuck his head round the door and told Mickey the news.

"Aw great!" groaned Mickey. "What about recording the babies, then?"

Shaz shrugged apologetically, murmured "See you," and trudged off. Titch was about to throw another stick for Raider when Mickey appeared, putting on his jacket. "Okay," he said. "That's that done. Let's not waste any more time." He closed the door and locked it, dropping the key into his pocket. Raider, delighted that he was not to stay on guard, ran round the three in mad circles as they walked into the wood. Night was falling as The Outfit reached Sycamore Thicket. A breeze stirred the tree-tops, making them whisper. They stopped and Jillo said, "D'you know what causes the wind, Mickey?"

Mickey shook his head. "No – what?"

"Trees moving about," said Jillo.

Mickey peered at her in the gloom. "You're crazy. It's the other way round."

"How d'you know?"

"Well, I – I just do, that's all."

"No, you don't. You only think you do. You can't prove it."

Mickey made an impatient noise and didn't answer. Titch found her sister's idea a bit creepy and shivered, trying not to think about it. It was creepy enough in Sycamore Thicket without that.

They gazed into the dark beneath the trees, listening. Raider, trained to utter obedience, stood absolutely still, sniffing the wind. There was nothing. No ghostly, luminous shapes. No phantom infants. No weeping. After a while, Jillo gulped and whispered, "We're not doing much good here. Are we going further in, or what?"

Mickey shrugged. "If you like. We could—" He broke off as Titch grabbed his sleeve, pointing. He followed her finger and saw a light moving between the trees. Raider began to growl and Mickey silenced him with a hiss.

Jillo looked at him. "What the heck is it, Mickey?" Not the babies, she prayed. Please don't let it be the babies. There was for her something particularly ghastly about the idea of phantom infants. Give me monsters every time, she thought.

Mickey shook his head. "Dunno. Listen."

They listened, straining their ears, but if there were sounds, they were drowned out by the wind. There was only the light – a little light which came and went between the haunted trees.

Presently Titch whispered, "Move towards it. Creep towards the light."

She started forward. Jillo grabbed her arm. "Are you crazy? We don't know what it is."

"We won't find out if we don't go and look," hissed Titch, squirming to free herself.

Mickey took her other arm. "Listen, Titch. You're a brave kid. We know that. You wouldn't be in The Outfit otherwise, but we've got to be careful here. We don't know what we're up against. If we go blundering in there now, we might find ourselves in the middle of something we can't handle."

He paused, peering into the gloom. "That light could be anything – vampires – aliens – anything. It might be completely harmless – a will o' the wisp or something, but we don't know. So what I suggest is, we call it a draw tonight and come back tomorrow when it's daylight and we've plenty of time. Okay?"

Jillo nodded. Titch shook off their hands and stood gazing towards the glimmer. They could tell she still wanted to investigate. They waited, and after a while she turned with a muttered "Okay," and led them out of the thicket.

6. Holes

Mickey was up early that Saturday morning. He always found it easier to get out of bed when he didn't have to go to school. The sun had pulled itself clear of the tree-tops and there wasn't a cloud in the sky. It was a bit nippy when Mickey stuck his nose outside, but he could tell it was going to warm up later.

"C'mon, Raider!" he cried. "Good brisk walk before breakfast."

It was October and in the woods the leaves were beginning to turn from green to gold, red and brown. Mickey walked quickly, using the network of narrow footpaths he knew so well, while Raider crashed about in the undergrowth seeking rabbits that weren't there. Their walk took them in a wide circle round the rim of the wood so they didn't go anywhere near Sycamore Thicket, which was in the middle. Mickey was saving that till the rest of The Outfit turned up.

It was still early when they got back to the caravan, so Mickey fried sausages and bacon for Raider and himself. Mickey ate his breakfast sitting on the step, while Raider sat on a chair and ate from his dish on the table. Jillo and Titch came before they'd finished and laughed at this arrangement. "Which of you's the dog?" asked Jillo.

"I am," growled Mickey, putting his plate on the step and picking up a sausage with his teeth.

Titch giggled. "I wish Dad would

feed the cows at table and put our breakfast in the field. It wouldn't matter about manners, then."

When Mickey and Raider had finished and the washing-up was done, they sat around waiting for Shaz. After a while, Jillo looked at her watch. "It's twenty-past nine," she said. "Perhaps he's not coming."

"Maybe his grandad's still in a mood," said Titch.

Mickey shook his head. "He'd let us know. He did last night, didn't he?"

They waited, and at twenty to ten Shaz came whistling along the path with his hands in his pockets. "Where've you been?" cried Jillo. "We've nearly grown roots waiting for you."

"Sorry," grinned Shaz. "Slept in. Hard work, cleaning house. You should try it sometime."

"I do it all the time!" protested Mickey.

"Yeah, but." Shaz nodded towards the caravan. "Your place is only an overgrown Coke can. You could clean it from end to end in ten minutes."

"Never mind arguing," put in Titch. "What about Sycamore Thicket?" She looked at Shaz. "Did you bring your recorder thing?"

"No!" Shaz shook his head. "No point. Ghosts don't come out in the daytime."

"Right." Mickey whistled for Raider, who was still looking for rabbits. "Let's go and see what there is to see."

In Sycamore Thicket, all was quiet. There was no wind, so the trees didn't whisper as they had last night. It was gloomy though, because the dense canopy of foliage shut out the sun, and the children felt shivery as they passed the badger set and headed for the middle where the moving light had been. Raider went before them, darting back and forth with his nose down, snuffling the damp ground. Presently he gave a single sharp yap and stood absolutely still. Mickey raised his hand to stop the others.

"What's up?" hissed Jillo.

"Dunno. Raider's found something. Wait here." He crept forward alone and saw that Raider was pointing his nose at a small mound of freshly turned soil. When he reached the spot he saw the hole from which the soil had been dug. It was about half a metre deep, and empty. He called the others.

"Who d'you reckon dug it?" asked Shaz. "And what's it for?"

"I think it's a grave," said Titch. "A man was here last night, digging it. We saw his light. Tonight he's going to murder his wife, bring her here rolled up in a carpet and bury her in this hole."

"You're a morbid little beast!" cried her sister. "You think of the most awful things. Anyway, graves are long and narrow. This hole's round."

"Well, maybe his wife's a little fat woman," Titch retorted.

"It might not be a grave," said Mickey. "But it could be somebody looking for a grave. An old one. The place where the babies are buried, for instance."

"Ugh!" Shaz pulled a face. "Who'd want to find a thing like that?"

Mickey shrugged. "Somebody who wanted to prove the old story true?" He shook his head. "Probably not. But somebody dug it, and if they dug it last night we have to ask ourselves why anyone would be digging a hole after dark in Sycamore Thicket."

"Badger-baiters?" suggested Jillo. Mickey shook his head.

"Not here. They'd dig into the set,

wouldn't they? No – there's an explan-
ation somewhere, but that's not it."

While the rest of The Outfit talked,
Raider continued to explore. Presently
he yapped again, and when Mickey
went to him he found that the lurcher
had sniffed out a second hole. It was
much the same as the first one, and
there was no clue as to its purpose.
There wasn't even a footprint in the
soft soil. The children walked backwards and forwards between the holes
for a while, comparing them, but there
was really nothing much to see.

"I know," said Titch. "Let's fill 'em
in and stamp 'em down so whoever's
digging them will have to start again."

"Trust you to dream up something
like that," cried Jillo. "You really are a
horrible little creepazoid, Titch."

"Well – it's our land and they're
digging without permission. It'd serve
'em right."

"It wouldn't solve the mystery though, would it?" said Mickey. "I think we should hide and keep watch – see if anybody comes."

"They won't come in daylight," said Shaz. "Not if they're up to something. And we can't stay out all night."

Mickey grinned. "Who can't?"

"Oh, well – I know you can if you want to – there's nobody to stop you, but you wouldn't, would you – not by yourself?"

"Dunno. Might. Have to see what happens, won't we? Let's hide."

They moved well away from the holes, stationed themselves behind a thick stand of trees, and settled down to watch.

7. Picnic

Nothing happened. Nobody came. After a while, Titch yawned and said, "This is really boring."

"Yeah," agreed Shaz. "Like watching chicken parts thaw."

"What d'you want to do, then?" asked Mickey.

"Anything," said Jillo. "How about walking down to the village and seeing what's happening?" Nothing ever happened in Lenton, but at least there'd be people and traffic and a few shop windows to look in.

"Okay." Mickey looked at Raider, who was lying with his muzzle on his paws and his eyes closed. "Walkies?"

The dog's eyes opened and he sprang erect, whining and wagging his tail. The children laughed and they set off, leaving the thicket and taking a footpath which would lead them down to the Lenton road.

They were almost there – could actually hear vehicles on the road – when Raider barked and went dashing ahead. Mickey, worried that he might run on to the road and be knocked down, called sharply, but for once Raider ignored him. Mickey set off after him at a trot, calling and whistling, and the others followed. Raider was barking at something, and, as they approached the edge of the wood, they heard voices and came upon an unexpected scene. A red Suzuki jeep was parked under the trees, and beside it on the grass sat two men with a car rug between them. On the rug was a coolbox and some plastic containers of sandwiches, salads and cold meats, and a bottle of mineral water. Raider was racing round and round the picnic, yapping and wagging his tail, while the two men watched him warily.

"Raider!" At the sound of his master's voice, the dog skidded to a halt and stood there panting, his tongue hanging out of his grin. "Come here, you daft mutt." Mickey's face was red with embarrassment. He made Raider sit and stay, then approached the men, who had got up. "I'm really sorry," he said. "I don't know what got into him – he's usually such a well-behaved dog. I hope he hasn't ruined your picnic?"

"Not at all." The elder of the two men, who was also the taller, smiled and shook his head. "We were a bit nervous, that's all – you hear so many stories these days about dog attacks."

Mickey nodded. "I know. Please – carry on with your meal. We're off now."

"No – don't go just yet." The man smiled again. "Sit down. Help yourselves to sandwiches – there are plenty. My friend and I are new to the area. I assume you all live locally?"

Mickey nodded. "Yes – we're all from Lenton. Are you and your friend on holiday?"

"Y-yes, that's right. We were wondering how this wood got its name. Weeping Wood. D'you know, by any chance?"

The children had settled themselves on the grass, but nobody took anything to eat. Jillo nodded. "Yes, I know. There's an old story that says sometimes, at night, you can hear babies crying in these woods."

"Babies?" The younger man looked quizzical. "You mean Babes in the

Wood – that sort of thing?"

Jillo shrugged. "Nobody knows how it started, but it's a very old story."

The man smiled. "It doesn't put you off playing here, then?"

Jillo shook her head. "Not really."

"You come here often?"

"Oh, yes. My parents own the wood."

"Oh, dear!" The man pulled a face. "Are we trespassing, then?"

Jillo chuckled. "No. Anyone can go in Weeping Wood, as long as they don't cause damage."

"Do a lot of people go there?"

"Quite a few, in summer." She grinned. "They avoid Sycamore Thicket, though."

"Why's that?"

"'Cause that's where the babies cry. The phantom babies."

"But surely they know it's just a tale?"

Jillo shrugged again. "People have

heard them. We have, as a matter of fact."

"You have?" The older man looked amazed. "When?"

"Couple of nights ago."

"You come here at night?" The man spoke sharply.

Mickey looked at him. "Yes we do. I live here, in a caravan. We sometimes go owl-spotting and badger-watching."

"Ooh." The man shook his head. "Not a good idea, that. Not where there are ghosts."

Mickey frowned. "How d'you mean? Ghosts can't hurt you, even if there are such things."

"Oh, but that's where you're wrong, young man. D'you know – I knew a fellow once, didn't believe in ghosts. Somebody told him a certain house was haunted and he said he'd spend the night there alone – prove it was all nonsense. So they locked him in and left him to it, and when they came in the morning to let him out, he was totally insane. His hair had turned white overnight and he was raving. Had to lock him up. He's there to this day as far as I know."

"Ugh!" Shaz shuddered. "Is that true?"

The man looked at him. "Certainly it is. I'm not in the habit of telling lies."

"Oh, no – I didn't mean –"

The man smiled. "That's quite all right. I know what you meant. It sounds incredible, but it's absolutely true, and there have been other incidents – some of them fatal. I'd steer well clear of – what d'you call it? – Sycamore Thicket, if I were you. In fact, I'd avoid the wood altogether after dark."

While the others had been talking, Titch had got up and walked slowly round the jeep. As she went on tiptoe to look inside, the younger man called sharply, "Come away from there, please!"

Titch shrugged and walked away from the vehicle, with a sheepish expression on her face. Jillo stood up, looking annoyed.

"We'll be off now," she said. "Take your litter with you when you go." She spun on her heel and strode into the wood.

Mickey and Shaz scrambled to their feet. Shaz looked wistfully at the un-touched sandwiches. Mickey said, "Sorry – about the dog. Have a nice day. C'mon, Raider."

They'd left the picnic well behind by the time they caught up with Jillo. "Hey, Jillo," protested Mickey, "that was a bit rude, wasn't it – what you said about the litter? Why'd you have to say that?"

"That man shouted at Titch," said Jillo. "She wasn't doing any harm.

Anyway, I didn't like them."

"They were okay," protested Shaz. "Offered us sandwiches and that. What was wrong with them?"

Jillo shook her head. "I dunno, Shaz. There was something about them, that's all. Two men, picnicking in the woods. That's unusual for a start. And then all their questions and that creepy story, and the warning about staying out of the woods at night. I think there's something not quite right about them."

"And I *know* there is," chirped Titch. They all looked at her.

"How d'you mean?" asked Mickey.

"Well," said Titch, enjoying their attention. "Just before that man shouted at me, I got a look inside the jeep, and do you know what I saw?"

"'Course we don't," snapped Jillo. "What did you see?"

"Metal detectors," said Titch.

8. This Very Night

"Metal detectors." Mickey looked at The Outfit, seated round him in Lenton's only café. Except for a pair of cyclists drinking tea at a corner table, they had the place to themselves. "That could mean a lot, or absolutely nothing."

Shaz looked at him. "What d'you mean?"

"Well – if they've been using the detectors in Sycamore Thicket, they might have dug the holes we found. That's what people with metal detectors do, isn't it? The detector tells them there's something made of metal underground, and they dig it up to see if it's valuable or interesting. But they might not have used the detectors there at all. From the way they were talking, it sounded as though they'd never seen the place before. They might just have been passing by, and decided Weeping Wood looked like a good spot to eat lunch."

"Hmmm!" Jillo looked dubious. "They might, but they knew it was called Weeping Wood, and there's no signpost or anything that says that. And they seemed very interested in the place. No – I reckon they made those holes, and for some reason they didn't want us to know about it."

"Okay." Mickey nodded. "Let's suppose they used their detectors in Sycamore Thicket and dug the holes. They could still be innocent treasure-hunters, couldn't they? I mean, we don't know when they dug them, do we? We've no proof they did it in the middle of the night. They might have done it in the daytime, for all we know."

"Yes," said Shaz, "but they were a bit secretive, and somebody was there during the night. We saw their lights."

"We saw lights," put in Titch. "But it could have been anybody. It could have been the ghosts, for all we know."

"I don't think so, Titch," said Jillo.

"They'd be secretive, even if they weren't up to anything," said Mickey. "You're supposed to have permission to use metal detectors on other people's land, and they haven't."

Jillo slurped up the dregs of her Coke and took her lips from around the straw. "Look," she said. "We could sit here arguing for ever. The point is, are we going to do anything, and if so, what?"

Mickey nodded. "Yes, of course we're going to do something – we're

The Outfit. What we need is a plan of action, and what I suggest is this." He sucked on his straw before continuing. "I suggest we keep Sycamore Thicket under constant surveillance till we actually see who's messing around in there and find out what they're doing."

"Constant?" Shaz frowned. "How can we do that, Mickey? We'd need to be out all night. Our folks wouldn't let us, and even if they did, when would we sleep?"

"This is an adventure!" cried Mickey. "You don't get people who have adventures worrying about sleep. I don't need sleep, anyway. We'll take turns watching, and I'll do the nights." He chuckled. "Unless Dad comes home."

"You mean you'll stay there by yourself?" gasped Titch. "In Sycamore Thicket? At night?"

Mickey nodded. "Sure. I was practically born in those woods, Titch.

I know every centimetre of 'em. I can see in the dark, and anyway I won't be alone. I'll have Raider."

"What about when we're at school?" asked Jillo.

"Ah, well – when I say constant surveillance, I don't mean in school time. I think these people, whoever they are, will operate after dark."

Shaz looked at him. "When do we start?"

Mickey grinned. "This very night, of course."

9. Today's Mystery Object

It was a quarter-past one when The Outfit left the café. Jillo and Titch had to hurry home for lunch. Shaz, Mickey and Raider walked with them as far as the bottom of the farm track before making their way to the caravan to eat sausage sandwiches. They were sharing a bar of chocolate for pudding when Shaz fished in his pocket and laid something on the table. "What d'you reckon that is?" he asked.

Mickey picked up the object. It was a small triangle of some orange-coloured substance which felt like stone. He shrugged. "Looks like a bit of pantile to me," he said.

Shaz frowned. "What's pantile?"

"Pantiles are those orange tiles they make roofs out of. You've seen 'em."

Shaz nodded. "I've seen 'em, but not around here. Lenton's all slate roofs."

"Where'd you find it?"

"Near one of those holes in the thicket. It'd been dug up."

"Hmm." Mickey turned the fragment, peering at it from all angles. "Wonder how it got there?"

Shaz pulled a face. "Maybe there was once a house with a pantile roof."

"In Sycamore Thicket? Don't talk daft. Who'd build a house in the middle of the woods?"

"The Three Bears?" suggested Shaz.

Mickey chuckled. "Oh, yeah. No – somebody must've carried it there at some time. Funny though. Here." He handed it to Shaz, who put it back in his pocket. They tidied up, put water down for Raider and went outside to wait for Titch and Jillo.

It was nearly three o'clock when the two girls appeared. "Where the heck did you go for lunch?" cried Mickey. "Hong Kong?"

"Sorry," said Jillo. "We were late and Dad made us tidy our room as a punishment. What have we missed?"

"Nothing much."

"Huh – I'll bet. What did you guys have for lunch?"

"Sausage sandwiches and chocolate."

"Lucky devils – I knew it'd be something like that. We had boring watercress soup and crusty boring rolls and fresh-fruit boring salad with boring yoghurt. It was dead boring."

Mickey nodded. "Sounds like it. You should have eaten with us – Shaz even gave us a touch of after-lunch entertainment with today's mystery object."

He looked at his friend. "Show 'em, Shaz."

"It's nothing really," protested Shaz. He dug in his pocket and brought out the orange fragment. The two girls looked at it.

"What is it?" asked Titch.

"Dunno," said Mickey. "That's why it's today's mystery object."

"I found it in the thicket," said Shaz. "Where the holes are. Mickey thinks it's a bit of roof-tile but the mystery is, how did it get there?"

"Who cares?" sneered Titch. "That's the rottenest mystery I've ever heard of."

Shaz shrugged. "I told you it was nothing."

"You were right," said Jillo. "It's very nearly as boring as watercress soup." She looked at Mickey. "Oughtn't we to be watching the thicket instead of inspecting bits of old roof? Kids who have adventures in books hardly ever inspect bits of old roof."

"Yeah," yawned Titch. "Let's go and watch that thicket before I die of excitement."

Mickey locked up the caravan and whistled for Raider. Shaz threw the bit of tile into some bushes and The Outfit set off to watch the thicket. It was a quarter-past three.

10. Faces

Towards dusk, a blustery wind began to shake the tree-tops and banks of dark cloud rolled in from the west. The children zipped up their jackets and hung on a while, but at seven o'clock it started to rain. Mickey squinted up at a patch of bruised-looking sky.

"I reckon it's set in for the night," he said. "We might as well pack it in. Nobody in their right mind'd come digging holes in this."

The others, bored anyway, nodded agreement. All except Raider, who preferred the outdoors whatever the weather, and who whined with disappointment when he realized he was going home. "We don't have to split up," said Mickey. "It's only seven. We can watch telly at my place."

They reached the caravan in the nick of time because, as Mickey unlocked the door, there was a flash of lightning and the rain began to fall really hard. "I hope this tin can you live in doesn't attract lightning," cried Jillo as they piled inside. She had to shout against the booming thunder.

"Never been struck yet," Mickey told her, stripping off his soggy jacket. "Where's Raider?"

"He ran off," said Shaz. "When you were unlocking the door."

"Daft animal," growled Mickey. "He'd rather drown than sit inside."

Except for the lightning, it was now quite dark. Mickey lit the gas fire and the lamps, and the children draped their jackets over chairbacks to dry. "What shall we do?" asked Titch.

Mickey shrugged. "What'd you like to do?"

"Computer games," Titch told him.

He chuckled. "Sorry, Titch. No can do. No electricity, see?"

"But there's a telly," Titch protested.

"Portable," said Mickey. "Batteries."

"Ah."

They sat down to watch telly, but the lightning was making the picture go funny, so Mickey turned it off and they played I-Spy while the wind rocked the caravan and rain drummed on the tin roof. Half an hour passed. Everybody was getting fed up with the game. They decided on one more round. It was Shaz's turn. "I spy," he said, "with my little eye, something beginning with EEEEEEAGH!"

"What the heck's up?" cried Mickey. Shaz was staring at the black, rain-streaked window behind his friend. "I saw – there was a face – a horrible face at the window."

"Don't talk daft!" Mickey twisted round to look. "There's nothing there now. You're just trying to—"

Titch's scream cut him off. She pointed to the glass panel in the door. Everybody looked. Pressed against the glass was a twisted, hideous face. As Mickey leapt to his feet it was withdrawn. He strode over to lock the door and found he'd left the key on the outside. He peered out, cupping his hands round his temples to cut reflection. He turned, shaking his head. "I can't see –" As he spoke, something outside began pounding on the caravan's metal wall and a face appeared briefly at the window.

"What – who are they?" cried Titch. "What are they doing?"

"Dunno." Mickey crossed to the

window and drew its curtain. "I can't lock us in 'cause the key's outside, so whatever they are, we'd better hope they stay out there." The pounding stopped, then started again in a different place.

"Go away!" cried Shaz. "We've called the police." A peal of maniacal laughter greeted his words and the pounding on the wall grew more fierce.

"They know there's no phone," said Mickey.

"I'm scared," moaned Shaz. "Those faces – they're not human. Remember what the guy said about ghosts – how they can drive you mad?"

"They're not ghosts!" cried Jillo. "Ghosts don't bang on walls."

"What are they, then?"

"Monsters!" croaked Titch. "They're monsters. Don't let 'em get in, Mickey."

"I can't stop 'em if they try the door, Titch. I don't half wish Raider was here. He'd see 'em off."

They huddled together in the middle of the tiny room, watching the door while the intruders banged and laughed, drowning out the sounds of the storm. The racket went on for several minutes, each minute seeming like an hour. Five times the hideous faces peered in through the door panel. Five times the children waited, sick with horror, for the door to burst open. And then, suddenly, it stopped. No more banging. No faces. No wild laughter. They listened for a few moments in silence. There was only the thunder, distant now, the hiss of rain on the roof and Raider somewhere, barking. Jillo gulped. "D'you think they've gone?"

Mickey shook his head. "Dunno. Maybe."

"D'you think Raider chased 'em off?" whispered Titch.

"No." Mickey shook his head. "Too far away. We'd better wait a bit."

Shaz gripped his arm. "Listen!"

"What?"

"Footsteps – can you hear 'em?"

Mickey ran his tongue over a dry lip. "Yeah."

"Jillo?" Titch reached out for her sister. Jillo wrapped her arms round her. They gazed at the door. The footsteps were closer now. Closer. A stair creaked. They could see something – a dark shape – through the glass. Titch whimpered. Something was scrabbling at the door, snuffling and growling.

It flew open.

11. Homecoming

"What's going on here?" The big man stood blinking in the light. Water dripped from the cycling cape he wore on to the carpet.

"Dad!" Mickey threw himself at the man and hugged him. "Are we glad to see you." The others smiled wanly at their friend's father as he frowned at them over Mickey's shoulder.

"What were you doing just now? I could hear your row from halfway up the farm track."

Mickey shook his head. "It wasn't us, Dad. There were some monsters or ghosts or something. Two of 'em, I think. They were running about outside, banging on the caravan and laughing, looking through the windows. They must've heard you coming and run off."

The big man laughed scornfully. "Monsters? Ghosts? There are no such things, Mickey. I thought I'd brought you up better than that."

"But we saw them, Dad." Mickey appealed to his friends. "Didn't we?"

Jillo nodded. "We did, Mr Wilbury. Honestly."

"They were horrible," Shaz confirmed.

"Big, ugly faces," said Titch.

"Village yobs," said Mr Wilbury. "That's who it'd be. They don't like folk who live in caravans."

"But their faces," protested Mickey. "They weren't human, Dad."

"Masks. They'd be wearing masks,

lad. They're cowards, people like them – they don't sign their names or show their faces and they run away when something bigger shows up." He looked around. "Where's Raider – he'd have seen 'em off like a shot."

Mickey pulled a face. "We don't know. We heard him barking, but he seemed a long way off."

"Hmm. Better go look for him, then. Silly mutt's probably got himself stuck in a rabbit hole or something." He looked at his son's friends. "What about you people – isn't it time you were thinking of going home? Your folks'll be wondering where you are."

Shaz shivered. "I can't say I fancy the walk," he said. "Even if those things were only people."

Jillo nodded. "I'm a bit like that myself."

Mr Wilbury nodded. "I can see you've all had a scare, and anyway, those idiots might still be skulking around somewhere, so I'll tell you what we'll do. We'll all go. Mickey and I will escort you through the wood and rescue that silly hound on our way back. How's that?"

The rain had slackened to a drizzle when they set off. They took Shaz to the High Street before trudging up the farm track to deliver Titch and Jillo. Mickey and his father then swung back into Weeping Wood to search for Raider. They'd searched for several minutes when Mickey's call was answered by a distant bark, and they steered themselves by a series of calls and barks till they found Raider, not stuck in a rabbit hole but tied by a length of electrical flex to a tree.

"I can't understand it," muttered Mr Wilbury as they tramped under dripping trees towards home. "Raider's a terror. If a stranger laid a hand on him, he'd have it off. They must've drugged him or something, but yobs don't do that – it's not their style."

Mickey was pretty sure his father was mistaken in believing the intruders had been village yobs. He'd been thinking hard, and now had a fair idea who they really were, but he wasn't going to say anything. That was Outfit business, and The Outfit would take care of it.

12. Footprints

They'd arranged to meet at the caravan at two o'clock on Sunday afternoon. It was a clear, cool day after the storm, and when Shaz arrived, the two girls were already there. "Hi, Shaz," greeted Jillo. "We're looking at footprints."

"Footprints?"

"Yes. Look." She indicated the patch of bare ground round the caravan steps. The rain had turned it to mud which was now drying out. In the mud were a great number of footprints. Some were their own – Shaz recognized the pattern of his trainers – and some were Raider's. There were deep, studded prints from Mr Wilbury's boots, but here and there you could see prints with a zig-zag pattern which hadn't been made by any of them.

"Dad says they're green welly prints," said Mickey. "Made by our monsters."

Shaz chuckled. "Monsters in green wellies?"

Mickey nodded. "That's right. The sort of monsters you find picnicking beside a jeep full of metal detectors."

Shaz looked at him. "Is that what your dad says?"

"No. He doesn't know about those guys. He thinks it was yobs from the village, but I reckon it was them."

"Hmmm." Jillo nodded. "Makes sense, on top of the warning they gave us. Trying to scare us so we'll stay away from whatever it is they're doing in Sycamore Thicket."

"They drugged Raider so they could tie him up. Even Dad says yobs wouldn't do that."

"So." Shaz frowned. "We're dealing with dangerous people. Ruthless people."

Mickey nodded. "Looks like it."

"Are we keeping watch tonight, then?"

Mickey shook his head. "Dad's nervous. Thinks the yobs might come back. He's keeping me in tonight."

"And what about tomorrow night?" said Shaz. "And the next night, and the one after that? Does this mean The Outfit's grounded – the adventure's over?"

"No!" Mickey laughed. "You don't know my dad. He's dead concerned today, but tomorrow or the next day he'll have forgotten all about it and he'll be off on his travels again, leaving Raider to mind me till he gets back."

"The rest of us could watch," suggested Titch.

"Our folks don't know anything happened last night."

Mickey shook his head. "Leave it, Titch, just for tonight. Let those guys think they've frightened us off." He smiled. "Give Dad's feet time to start itching again, then he'll be off and we can do anything we like."

They passed the afternoon by taking Raider for a long walk, while Mr Wilbury worked on the caravan roof. Last night's storm had revealed a small leak and he wanted the place weather-proof for the coming winter. They made a point of staying well away from Sycamore Thicket in case the two mysterious strangers were watching them, and long before dusk they split up and went their separate ways.

If they've been watching, mused

Mickey, hurrying home, they won't expect any more trouble from us. They'll think we're terrified. They think we're just a bunch of kids, but they're wrong. We're The Outfit.

13. Interest

"Can you all stop what you're doing for a minute?" Mickey looked up. Mrs Latimer was holding two pieces of thick cardboard which had been bent to form the pitched roof of an L-shaped building. Gordon Spilsbury was standing beside her. When she had everybody's attention, the teacher held up the pieces of cardboard.

"Gordon's group is nearly ready to put the roof on the villa," she said. "And Gordon has just asked me what colour it should be." She smiled. "Can anybody tell him?" Her eyes moved from face to face but the children either looked down or shook their heads and murmured, "No, Miss."

"Think about the pictures we've looked at. What colour were the roofs in those?" Some of the children risked a sidelong glance at the picture Gordon's group was working from, but it was in black and white. Mrs Latimer shook her head. "Short memories," she scolded. "They were red, or reddish brown, because the Romans used terracotta pantiles for their roofs."

Interest stirred in Mickey's brain. Terracotta pantiles. Shaz had found a bit of pantile in Sycamore Thicket, and had suggested that maybe there had once been a house there. What if – ? He stuck up his hand.

Mrs Latimer looked at him. "Yes, Michael?"

"Did the Romans have any villas

around here, Miss?"

The teacher shook her head. "We don't know, Michael. There was the fort, of course – the one we went to look at a few weeks ago – but if there were villas, no trace of them has ever been found.

Why do you ask?"

"Just wondered, Miss."

At breaktime, Mickey tracked down Shaz in the yard. "What did you do with that bit of orange stuff you found?" he asked.

Shaz shrugged. "I chucked it away. Nobody was interested."

"Well, I'm a bit interested now. D'you think you could find it again?"

"Dunno. It went in the bushes behind the caravan. I could look I suppose, but it was very small."

"We'll both look," said Mickey. "Tonight. Titch and Jillo too."

"Maybe Raider could sniff it out for

us," grinned Shaz. "But why the sudden interest?"

Mickey winked. "Tell you tonight," he promised.

14. Diddums

Shaz was first to arrive at the caravan. It was half-past six. Mickey and Raider had finished tea and were sitting on the step.

"Hi, Shaz!" greeted Mickey.

"Hi, Mickey, Raider." Shaz looked around. "Where's your dad?"

"What – Raider's or mine?"

"Yours, you div."

Mickey grinned. "Guess."

"Umm – gone off again?"

"Right first time!"

"I thought I didn't see his old truck back there. Where's he gone?"

Mickey shrugged. "Don't ask me.

And don't ask me when he'll be back, either."

"Wasn't going to," smiled Shaz. "I was going to ask why you're interested in that bit of tile I found."

"I'll tell you when the others come," said Mickey. "And in the meantime, let's see if we can find it."

They spent the next twenty minutes crawling about under the bushes behind the caravan. Raider sniffed and rooted as though he knew what they were looking for, but nothing turned up. They were about to abandon the search when the girls arrived.

"What're you doing?" cried Jillo. "Slug hunting?"

Shaz backed out on his knees and stood up, knocking dirt and bits of twig off himself with his hands. "We were looking for something I threw in there," he said, "but it's hopeless."

Mickey emerged, looking even more

tousled than usual. Raider continued to search. Mickey told the girls what they'd been seeking. Titch looked at him. "What d'you want to find that for?"

"That's what I want to know," grumbled Shaz.

Mickey told them what Mrs Latimer had said about Roman roofs.

"Are you saying you think there was once a Roman villa in Sycamore Thicket?" said Shaz.

Mickey shrugged. "Why not? There could have been, couldn't there?"

"S'pose so." Shaz frowned. "But wouldn't somebody know about it?" He looked at Jillo. "Your mum and dad – they own the place. Wouldn't they know?"

Jillo shook her head. "They might not. You sometimes hear of villas being discovered, and they've been there centuries without anyone knowing."

"Yes," cried Titch. "And Sycamore

Thicket's haunted. Nobody goes there, or they didn't till those two men came along. A villa could have stayed hidden there for ever."

"So." Jillo looked at Mickey. "What were you going to do with the bit of tile?"

"I thought I'd take it along to the museum. There's a man there – an archaeologist – who knows all about Roman stuff. He came to the fort with our class and showed us around. He'd know if that bit of tile was Roman."

"Yes, and what if it was?" demanded Jillo. "He'd want to know where you got it, right? And when you told him he'd want to have a look, and then if there's anything there he'd have people all over the thicket, digging." She pulled a face. "Bang goes our adventure."

"Hmmm," said Mickey. "Never thought of that."

"Thicko," growled Titch.

"Hey – watch it, you!" Mickey pretended he was about to thump her. Titch giggled and dodged. Raider burst out of the bushes with a rotting stick in his jaws.

"Oh, well done, Raider!" cried Shaz. "Just what we need – a filthy bit of rotten wood."

"Anyway," said Mickey. "We don't have the fragment now, so that's out. The thing is, what do we do next?"

"Well," said Jillo. "Let's see. What do we know? We know that two strangers are interested in Sycamore Thicket. They've got metal detectors and they've dug holes. If there was a villa it might explain their interest, but we know they're not proper archaeologists because they work in the middle of the night and they've tried to scare us away." She looked at Mickey. "So what we need to know is, two things. First, we need to know if there was once a villa in the thicket. That means we have to go in there and make a thorough search. And second, we need to know what the two strangers are after. If they've found a villa, why don't they announce their discovery instead of sneaking around in the dark?"

"Hmmm." Mickey nodded. "You're right, Jillo. This is our adventure and we'll keep it to ourselves, and the first thing is to get a long look at Sycamore Thicket in daylight. In fact," he grinned, "I wouldn't be surprised if a certain kid's missing from school tomorrow. You know – upset tummy, and no mum to look after him?"

"Aaah," crooned Shaz. "Who could blame him, poor little thing?"

"Shame," sighed Jillo.

"Diddums," murmured Titch.

They burst out laughing, and Raider looked at them as though they'd all gone mad.

15. Stones

Mickey was in no hurry Tuesday morning. He lay in bed till a quarter-to nine thinking about Jillo, Titch and Shaz going to school. When he finally got up he grilled pepperoni pizzas for Raider and himself and they sat on the step, munching and watching the leaves turn brown. It was ten o'clock when Mickey set off for Sycamore Thicket, leaving Raider in charge of security.

He moved cautiously as he entered the thicket, but it was deserted and there were no new holes. He didn't really know what he was looking for, but he began walking very slowly, examining the ground in front of him. Presently he saw the corner of a stone sticking up out of the leaf-mould. He hacked at it with the toe of his trainer, hoping to loosen it so he could pick it up but it wouldn't budge. "Big 'un," he grunted, going down on his knees and scraping earth from around it with his fingers. He knew that if he could find the bottom of the stone, he'd be able to get his fingers under it and prize it loose. Four centimetres down he did find it, but he couldn't get his fingers underneath because the stone seemed to be standing on top of another one.

Mickey found a short, thick stick and used it to scrape soil from around this second stone. When the hole was about ten centimetres deep he came to the bottom of this stone and there underneath was another. He got right down and laid his cheek on the ground, peering at the crack between the top stone and the next. It was filled with a layer of some black stuff which felt coarse and grainy when he ran a finger along it. He sat back on his heels and frowned. Three flattish stones, one on top of another, with some sort of mortar between. It reminded him of something he'd seen recently, but where?

A stab of excitement made him gasp as the answer came to him. Of course! The fort. The remains of the Roman fort his class had visited a few weeks ago. There hadn't been much left of it – the foundations of some buildings and a few bits of standing wall, but in one place the archaeologists had un-covered a hypocaust. The floor which had once lain above the hypocaust was gone but the short, stubby pillars which had supported this floor were still there – several rows of them – and they were made out of flat stones piled on top of one another with mortar between. The man from the museum had told them that, over the centuries, the pillars had become covered with soil and so had remained undiscovered for one and a half thousand years. And this pile of stones he'd begun to uncover looked very like the ones at the fort – Mickey bet if he went on digging the pile would turn out to be about sixty centimetres tall and roughly square in section. He couldn't do it, of course – he'd need proper tools – but he didn't need to. He'd come hoping to find proof that there was once a Roman villa in Sycamore Thicket, and he'd done it, right? Of course, his pile of stones might turn out to be the remains of a far more recent structure – a medieval pigsty perhaps – but Mickey doubted it. The stones were right, the mortar was the same – it just had to be the pillar of a hypocaust. He grinned, rubbing his hands together to get the soil off them. Wait till I tell the others, he thought. They'll be amazed.

He stood up and was knocking leaf-mould off his jeans when a voice behind him growled, "And just what do you think you're playing at, sonny?"

16. Danger Zone

Mickey spun round, to find one of the two Suzuki picnickers glaring at him. He was wearing a camouflage flak jacket and carrying a metal detector. "I – er – I was just messing about. I found a bit of an old building."

The man nodded. "You would. There was an army post here in the First World War."

"An army post?"

"Yes. This is no place for you to be messing about in – it's a danger zone."

"Why?"

"Because of the mines."

"Mines?" said Mickey. "What sort of mines?"

The man's laugh was like a bark. "Land-mines," he said. "Unexploded ones. There are shells too, and grenades. That's why my colleague and I are here. The Ministry of Defence has employed us to clear up the explosives and make the area safe."

Mickey gulped. "I didn't know. Nobody knows. Why aren't there signposts? Why isn't it fenced off?"

The man shrugged. "It was a very small post, and a long time ago. I suppose the army forgot about it."

"But they've remembered now?" Mickey wasn't sure he believed this man. In his flak jacket, he looked like somebody who might have come from the Ministry of Defence, and his story about the mines would certainly explain the digging and the metal detectors, but there was something fishy about it, all the same.

The man nodded. "That's right. They've remembered, and a good job for you they have. You could have been blown to bits at any second."

"I'd better go, then." Mickey wondered where the other man was. He wished Raider was here. He began to move away.

"Stand still!" The man was staring at the ground by Mickey's feet. "You can't tread just anywhere in here. You'd better follow me, and be very careful indeed."

The man set off, moving slowly, sweeping the ground in front of him with the metal detector. Mickey followed gingerly, treading in his footsteps. He felt scared. Really scared. He'd seen videos where people trod on mines. A flash and a bang and there's nothing left – just a smoking hole in the ground. The walk to the edge of the thicket seemed to take for ever, but they made it at last. Mickey slumped against a tree and let out a long breath. His knees were trembling and he felt sick.

The man looked at him. "You're all right," he said. "It's safe here, but don't you so much as set foot in this thicket again till we're through clearing it, d'you understand?"

Mickey nodded. "How will we know?"

"Know what?"

"When it's clear."

"It'll be in the paper. Off you go – and don't forget to tell your friends."

The man went back into the thicket. Mickey watched him. He was using exactly the same path they'd come out by. Mickey shivered, thinking of all the times he and Raider had crossed that ground. He still wasn't sure he believed the man's story, but one thing was certain – no member of The Outfit would enter Sycamore Thicket again till he'd checked it out.

17. Porkies

"Mrs Latimer sent for me," said Shaz that evening, when they were all sitting in the caravan. "She asked if I knew why you weren't at school." He grinned. "I said you told me you might not be in today and that you mentioned your tummy. It wasn't a lie, was it?"

Mickey shook his head. "Not exactly. Thanks, Shaz."

"So," said Titch. "What did you discover while we were slaving away in school?"

Mickey smiled grimly. "You'll be amazed." He told them about finding the pillar of stones, how he'd been surprised by the man in the flak jacket, and the man's story about the army post. When he'd finished he looked at Jillo. "I want you to do something, Jillo. Right now."

"What?"

"I want you to go home and ask your dad if there was ever an army post in Sycamore Thicket."

Jillo shook her head. "I don't think there was. My dad's family has owned this land for over a hundred years and I've never heard anybody mention an army post, but I'll go and ask."

"Be careful how you ask," warned Mickey. "We don't want your dad to know about the mysterious strangers or he'll stop us investigating."

Jillo nodded. "I'll be careful." She slipped away, leaving Titch with the others. They waited.

* * *

It was twenty minutes before Jillo came back, out of breath. She flopped down in an easy chair and shook her head. "Dad says there never was an army post." She chuckled. "I told him we found an old tin hat in there. He said some people dump their rubbish just anywhere."

"So," murmured Mickey. "That guy was telling me porkies. I thought so."

"Porkies?" queried Titch.

Jillo smiled. "Pork pies, Titch – lies." Titch giggled.

"So we know there was a villa in the thicket," said Shaz, "and that those men know about it. We don't know what they're doing, and they've made it pretty obvious they don't want us to find out." He grinned. "I vote we do our best to find out before we tell anybody."

Jillo nodded. "So do I."

"Me too," said Titch.

Mickey nodded. "We're all agreed, then – even though it's likely to be dangerous?"

"'Course!" cried Shaz. "This is The Outfit you're talking to, remember?"

"I'd like to talk to the man at the museum," said Mickey, thoughtfully. "The one who showed my class the fort. Trouble is, the museum shuts at four-thirty. We'd never make it after school."

"There's Saturday," said Jillo.

"I know, but today's only Tuesday. It'd be nice to talk to him before Saturday."

Shaz smiled. "How's your tummy, Mickey?"

Mickey pulled a face. "Not much better, Shaz. I reckon it could be Thursday before I'm fit enough for school."

"Oooh, at the earliest," said Jillo. "You don't want to pass your bug on to some other kid, do you?"

"That'd be a rotten thing to do," scolded Titch.

"You're right," groaned Mickey. "I love school. In fact I feel miserable whenever I'm not there, but I must force myself to stay away tomorrow. It's my duty."

Jillo nodded gravely, then burst out laughing. "You really are a lucky beggar, Mickey, being able to please yourself. Come on – let's do the oath." They formed their circle round Raider and squatted.

"Faithful, fearless, full of fun,
Winter, summer, rain or sun,
One for five and five for one –
THE OUTFIT!"

18. Mr Jackson

At ten o'clock on Wednesday morning, Mickey strolled across the park to the museum. Just inside the door a man in uniform sat behind a desk.

"Excuse me," said Mickey.

"Yes?"

"Is Mr Jackson in?"

"Yes."

"Can I see him?"

"Expecting you, is he?"

"No."

"What d'you want him for?"

"He showed my class the Roman fort. I've got a question for him."

The man sighed. "Mr Jackson's very

busy, y'know. Wait here." He went off along a gloomy corridor.

Mickey waited, and presently the man reappeared, beckoning. "Come this way, son." Mickey followed him along the corridor till he stopped by an open door. "This is the young man, sir," he said, steering Mickey through the door way. Mickey found himself in a large, book-lined office.

Mr Jackson smiled across a cluttered desk. "Thank you, Bert." The man withdrew, closing the door. Mr Jackson nodded towards a chair in front of the desk. "Sit down, and tell me your name."

"It's Michael, Mr Jackson. Michael Wilbury."

"I understand you have a question to ask me, Michael."

"Yes, please. It's about the Romans."

"Ah-ha." Mr Jackson nodded.

"Well, at school we're making models

of Roman things, and one group's doing a villa, and I was wondering whether there were any villas round here."

"Ah, well now." Mr Jackson smiled. "That's an interesting question, Michael, and the answer is, nobody knows. No trace of a villa has ever been found in this area, but there's a story that, when the local Britons rose in revolt against the Romans in the year 229, a retired general fled to the fort with his family and servants for protection. Now that general was a very wealthy man, and his home would certainly have been a villa. If he fled to the fort, his villa can't have been very far away, and yet as I said, no trace has ever been uncovered." He smiled again. "Trouble is, Michael, we're not even sure the story's true. The general certainly existed, and we know the revolt actually happened, but the story goes on to tell of buried treasure – a fabulous hoard, supposedly buried by the general in the garden of his home before he fled, and tales of this sort are always suspect."

At the mention of buried treasure, Mickey's heart kicked him in the chest. He swallowed hard, trying to keep his excitement from showing on his face. When Mr Jackson stopped speaking, he said, "Could it be true, though – about the treasure?"

Mr Jackson chuckled. "It could, Michael. Hoards have been found from time to time in other areas. All I'm saying is that there are hundreds of tales about buried gold – fairy gold, Viking gold, pirate gold, royal gold – all supposedly true, yet none of these treasures ever comes to light." He leaned back in his chair and began to fill a pipe with tobacco.

"Wouldn't he have come back for it when the revolt was over – the general,

I mean?" Mickey said.

Mr Jackson lit up and shook his head behind a cloud of smoke. "The Britons overran the fort," he said. "Killed everybody in there, including the general, if he was ever there at all." He looked at Mickey. "Why are you so interested in villas, Michael?" He chuckled. "Haven't found one, have you?"

Mickey's heart kicked again, even though he knew the man was joking. He gulped, then grinned. "No, sir. I just wondered, that's all."

Mr Jackson pressed a bellpush on his desk and stood up. "Well, Michael – thank you for coming to see me. I'm only sorry I wasn't able to be more helpful."

"Oh, you've been very helpful, Mr Jackson," said Mickey, almost bursting with excitement. He couldn't wait to tell the others what he'd found out. There was a knock on the door and

Bert looked in. Mr Jackson held out his hand for Mickey to shake.

"Goodbye, Michael," he said. "Bert will show you out."

Dawdling through the park, Mickey looked at his watch. Twenty-past ten. "Nearly eight hours before I see the others," he groaned. "Roll on." He decided he'd take a look at Sycamore Thicket. It would help to pass the time.

19. Barmy

"What I found out yesterday was peanuts," bragged Mickey, "compared with what I've found out today."

He hadn't been able to wait for The Outfit to assemble at the caravan. Instead, he'd taken the risk of meeting them as they came out of school. None of the teachers had spotted him, and now the four friends were dawdling along the High Street. Mickey told them what Mr Jackson had said about the general and his treasure.

"Don't you see?" he cried. "If the general's villa was in Sycamore

Thicket, it'd explain everything – the holes in the ground – everything. It all fits. Those two guys have found the villa, and they're after the hoard. If they worked openly they'd have to hand over anything they found to the authorities. As it is, they could just disappear with the stuff and nobody would know."

"They could," grinned Shaz, "if it wasn't for – da-daa – The Outfit!"

"Right," nodded Mickey. "And if we're right about all this, we know what we're up against. Those guys have a fortune within their grasp. They're not going to abandon it because of a bunch of kids."

Jillo swallowed hard. "So it's really dangerous, what we're doing?"

Mickey nodded. "Yes, so if you'd rather let your folks in on it now, I wouldn't blame you. After all, the treasure, if there is one, is on their land. The courts might decide it belongs to them."

"I don't think we should let anybody in on it," interrupted Titch. "Not till we've solved the mystery. Let's watch 'em actually find the treasure, then tell Mum and Dad."

Mickey shrugged. "Fine, if it's okay with the rest of you." He grinned. "It might not be long either. I was in the thicket a couple of hours ago. There are more holes now, and they've marked out a little square of ground with pink tape."

"Was anybody about?" asked Jillo.

"Not a soul. I was very careful, I can tell you."

"And what was in the little square?" Shaz enquired.

Mickey shook his head. "Dunno. I didn't cross the tape – I suppose I was still thinking about land-mines. But I wouldn't be surprised if that's where they think the treasure is. I vote we watch tonight, and I bet they'll be digging up that square."

They came to the farm track, where their ways parted. "Six o'clock?" asked Mickey. "My place?"

The two girls nodded and Shaz said, "Six."

Mickey winked. "You're barmy," he said. "The lot of you."

20. Crazy

It was six-fifteen when The Outfit approached Sycamore Thicket. The sun hung low in the western sky, but it would not set for another hour. The children were tense with the feeling that their adventure was approaching its climax. Even Raider felt it, dashing about in the greenish gloom, sniffing and yipping till Mickey brought him to heel. They'd come to where they could just see a corner of the square with its pink tape. There was nobody about.

"We'll watch from here," Mickey whispered. "They probably won't come till dark, but when they do, there's to be no talking – not even in whispers. They might think they've scared us off with that land-mine story, but they'll be jumpy all the same."

"What do we do if they find the treasure?" asked Shaz.

"We move," said Mickey. "Fast, to Jillo's place. We have to fetch her dad before those guys can get the stuff out of the ground and into their jeep. Watch for my signal."

"I've got a better idea," said Jillo.

"What?"

"Well, we can only just see the place from here in broad daylight. In the dark it's going to be virtually impossible. We'll see their lights, but we might not know they've found something till they start lifting it out. I think one of us should get a lot closer – close enough to hear what they're saying – and signal to the others as soon as the men start getting excited."

Mickey looked at her. "You're crazy. If you were any closer they'd spot you in no time."

"Not if I was up that tree." She pointed to an ancient sycamore whose branches reached out over the tape. Mickey shook his head.

"You can't do that, Jillo. You'd be right on top of them. They'd hear you breathing."

"No, they wouldn't. I'd have my white hanky out, and when I waved it you'd know it was time to go for Dad."

"You're crazy. You might as well go and sit in that square till they show up, then say 'Hi – is it all right if I watch?'"

"Mickey's right, Jillo," said Shaz. "It's too dangerous."

"I don't want to lose you," said Titch. "Even if you are a pain."

"Well, I'm doing it," insisted Jillo, "whatever you say." She pulled the handkerchief from her pocket, stuffed it up her sleeve and moved towards the ancient sycamore. The others watched her, thinking, she won't do it. Not really. Any second now she'll chicken out and come back, and I won't blame her.

She didn't come back. She paused briefly and turned to hiss, "Watch for the hanky." Then she went on. They watched her climb into the lower branches and look their way, settling herself where they could see her. She was lying like a leopard along a great, thick branch, relying on the foliage beneath her to hide her from the strangers when they should come. Mickey let out a long breath and shook his head. "Crazy," he said. They hid and waited.

21. Capture!

Jillo saw them first and twisted round on her perch, stabbing the air with a finger to show her friends where the men were coming from. It was so dark now under the trees that they could scarcely see her. Mickey waved back and hissed a warning at Raider to be quiet.

The three children crouched behind their chosen trees and gazed towards the tape, now virtually invisible. A bobbing light and muted voices told them the strangers were close. A twig cracked, and two shadowy figures came flitting between the trees. They stopped under Jillo's perch and stood a moment, muttering. Mickey wondered whether Jillo could hear what they were saying. The men then moved apart and there came a succession of furtive sounds – clinking, scraping and a single sharp click. Immediately after the click, the air became filled with the plaintive cries of infants in distress.

"What the heck –" Shaz was on his feet.

"Ssssh!" Mickey grabbed him. "For pete's sake get down, Shaz."

"Mickey." Titch's eyes were like saucers. "It's the phantoms. I'm scared."

Mickey shook his head. "That click. It's a cassette. They've got a tape of babies crying, that's all." And that's what we heard the other night, he thought. There are no phantoms, after all. He stuffed a fist in his mouth to keep from laughing out loud with relief.

The men were digging – working furiously. The children could hear the chock and scrape of spades through the recorded howls of the babies. The men were so intent now, and there was so much noise that The Outfit could afford to breathe normally and even move their cramped limbs. Mickey had time to wonder how the two strangers had got their cassette. Probably rounded up a bunch of babies and stuck pins in 'em, he told himself. Anyway, those guys aren't keeping any sort of a look-out, so the rest of the job should be easy.

No sooner had he told himself this than Jillo fell out of her tree.

After that, things happened very quickly. One of the men yelled a warning to the other and threw himself at Jillo, who was attempting to stand up. Titch, seeing her sister in danger, broke cover and pelted towards the men, shrieking at the top of her voice. Raider saw no reason why he should be the only one to keep quiet and raced after her, barking furiously. The second man grabbed Titch by the hair and was jerking her head this way and that when Shaz and Mickey cannoned into him, knocking him over.

It was a short struggle. When it was over, all four children lay panting on the ground, arms and feet tightly bound with pink tape. The two strangers, sweaty and dishevelled, stood glaring down at them. The cassette player continued to churn out the howls of ill-used infants, and of Raider there was no sign at all.

22. Raider

Raider had a pretty good brain, as dog brains go. He knew his friends were in trouble and needed help. He also knew that if he stayed around, the strangers would use the gun they'd used on him before – the gun which stung like a wasp, then made him fall asleep. So, as the other members of The Outfit were overpowered and trussed, Raider ran off through the thicket.

He didn't know what to do. For a while he lay under a fallen tree, listening to the sounds the strangers made. The babies weren't weeping any more but the digging continued, and Raider decided the men must have buried a particularly juicy bone here at some time. He could see their flashlights coming and going, and wondered miserably what was happening to Mickey and the others. A picture of Mr Wilbury came into his mind and he thought, that's it. I'll find Mr Wilbury. He'll know what to do. He got up and headed for the caravan, loping through the shadows with lolling tongue.

The caravan was locked. No light showed in its windows. Mr Wilbury's scent was faint and stale. Raider circled the place, yipping and whining, but nobody came. He sat down under the steps with his muzzle on his forepaws and gazed into the dark.

Time passed. Raider, uneasy in his mind, dozed and woke, dozed and woke. He was waiting for Mr Wilbury, who at that moment was sitting in a pub a hundred miles away with no plan to come home. Presently, the dog's sharp ears detected footfalls approaching through the trees. A picture of the strangers, whose stale scent was mingled here with the scent of his friends, flicked across his mind, and he growled softly. A thin beam of light glanced off the caravan's metal skin as a man came out of the trees with a torch.

"Hello?" The man strode forward, calling. Raider knew his voice. He was Mr Wilbury's friend from the farm. Raider came out from under the steps, barking and wagging his tail. The torch light made him flinch. "Raider." The man bent to him, ruffled the coarse hair on his neck. "Where is everybody, eh? Where've they gone, boy?" Raider detected anxiety in his tone – an anxiety which matched his own. Here was help. Help for Mickey and the others. He turned, trotted a short way and looked back, whining.

"What is it, Raider?" the man asked. "D'you know where the kids are? Is that it?" Raider barked and repeated his action, and the man said, "Go on then, boy – show me!" Raider barked and set off for Sycamore Thicket, looking back from time to time to make sure the farmer was following.

23. It's Not On

The diggers struck the hoard at nine o'clock. The trussed children, propped against the trunk of Jillo's tree, heard a stifled exclamation and saw their captors link arms and caper round the hole, laughing and whooping. "They've got it," murmured Mickey. "Now what will they do with us?"

The dance of triumph was brief. When it was over the two men muttered together, then separated. One hurried off through the trees. The other came across to the children.

"Well," he smirked. "That's that.

There's a king's ransom at the bottom of that hole. My colleague will fetch the jeep, we'll load up and be three hundred miles away by dawn." He smiled unpleasantly. "Which leaves only one problem."

"What to do with us," said Shaz.

The man nodded. "Exactly. There are several options, none of which would be much fun for you, I'm afraid, but then, if you will go poking your revolting little noses into things which don't concern you, what can you expect?" He smiled again. "We could leave you here, where your cries might bring rescue, unless of course they were mistaken for the cries of phantom infants." He chuckled. "What d'you think of our little cassette, by the way? Clever, or what?" He didn't wait for a reply, but went on. "Or we could take you with us and dump you at the roadside a hundred miles away at three in the morning. Or – and this is my own personal favourite – we could knock you on the head with our spades and bury you right here. There's a perfectly good hole, you see, and it seems a pity to waste it." He shrugged. "Luckily for you, my colleague's not nearly as ruthless as I am, so I suspect we'll end up leaving you here, which is better than you deserve." He cocked his head, listening. "I do believe that's him now." He grinned. "Devil of a job, you know, driving between these trees. Still, it's only once, isn't it?"

"You won't get away with it," said Titch.

The man laughed. "There's not a lot you can do to stop us, is there, tied up as you are?"

"You haven't got us all," grated Mickey. "There's Raider. He'll do something, you'll see." The man turned, laughing, and strode towards the jeep's bucking headlamps as the vehicle approached.

Jillo looked at Mickey. "Do you really think Raider will do something?"

Mickey shrugged in his bonds. "Dunno. I was trying to worry him." He nodded towards the jeep, which had stopped. "It'll be too late anyway. Look."

The driver had left the engine running, and the two men were moving to and fro between the jeep and the hole, carrying a variety of objects which the children couldn't see clearly, but which seemed heavy. It was obvious that, within the next few minutes, the hole would have surrendered all of its treasures and the men would be gone.

It was at that moment that the children heard Raider's bark. The men heard it too. One of them hissed,

"Damn!" and the other said, "Where's the dart gun?" He was leaning into the jeep to get it when Raider burst from the trees, grabbed his trouser-leg and tugged. The man, half off balance, staggered sideways and fell, dropping the gun. The children cheered, and Mickey cried, "Good boy, Raider – go get 'em, lad!" Raider turned, snarling, towards the second man, who grabbed a spade and raised it above his head. "Call him off," he cried, "or I'll cut him in two!"

At once a voice boomed. "Oh, no, you won't!" and the children shrieked with joy as farmer Denton loomed out of the dark.

The man cursed, whirled and ran towards the captives. "Stand still," he yelled, "or one of these kids gets it!" The children cringed as he stood over them, the spade raised high above his head. The farmer skidded to a halt and stood panting, watching him. "If you so much as—" he began, but the man's voice cut him off. "Raymond – get in the jeep." He looked at the farmer. "We're taking one kid – the little one. Don't try to stop us, or else!" Without taking his eyes off her father, he stooped and yanked Titch to her feet. Half-carrying her, and with the spade in his hand, he began moving towards the vehicle, watching the farmer the whole time.

Raider attempted another attack on the driver, but the man had recovered the dart gun and Denton called him off. The man was half-in and half-out of the jeep when the babies began to cry.

The second man, approaching the jeep with the struggling Titch, cried, "Turn that damn thing off, you fool!"

His friend stuck his head out. "It's n-not on," he croaked.

"Huh?" The man glanced wildly about him. "B-but it must be – there's no such thing as a—" Titch felt his grip slacken and kicked backwards with all her strength. Her heel caught him just below the kneecap, causing him to stagger. He flung out his arms for balance and she was free. The jeep was moving – bucking and swerving as the driver crouched over the wheel, his friend forgotten. The man flung his spade aside and ran after the vehicle, but the farmer brought him down with a flying tackle and the two of them watched from the ground as the jeep rammed a tree and stalled.

At the first infant wail, the cheers of The Outfit had frozen in their throats. Raider stood trembling with his tail between his legs, too cowed to bark. The driver slumped unconscious over his wheel and the two men on the ground lay winded. Seconds before, the dank air of Sycamore Thicket had rung to many sounds. Now, the tiny phantoms had it all to themselves.

24. Fantastic

It was the first day of the Christmas holidays. An icy wind rocked the leafless trees of Weeping Wood, but inside the caravan it was snug and warm. Four members of The Outfit sat round the fire, sipping hot chocolate and talking. Much had happened since that hectic night in Sycamore Thicket, so they had plenty to talk about. The fifth member was chasing rabbits in the woods but that was up to him, and anyway he had a coat of thick hair to keep him warm.

"So the story was true, after all," said Mickey. "Mr Jackson was amazed.

He said tales of buried treasure are almost always just tales."

"Have they finished excavating?" asked Shaz.

Jillo nodded. "They pulled out the day before yesterday, but they've fenced off the site and Dad says they'll be back next spring. He thinks the villa will become a tourist attraction eventually."

Mickey pulled a face. "I hope not. Who wants crowds of people all over the place?"

Shaz shrugged. "It's the price of fame, Mickey."

"Yes!" cried Titch. "And we were famous for a while, weren't we, Shaz? Our pictures in the paper. All that."

"What about the hoard?" asked Mickey. "Have they decided who it belongs to yet?"

Jillo shook her head. "Not yet, but Dad says it's bound to be declared treasure trove, which means he and

Mum will get a big reward."

"And what about us?" demanded Titch. "The Outfit? We cracked the secret, didn't we? We had all the danger."

Jillo nodded, smiling. "Don't worry, Titch – we're not forgotten. Mum says if they get the reward they'll build us the best gang hut in the world."

Shaz looked at Jillo. "Is that true – we'll have our own headquarters?"

"That's what Mum said."

"Fantastic!" Shaz's eyes shone. "Won't that be fantastic, Mickey?"

Mickey nodded. "Yeah – fantastic."

"You don't sound very enthusiastic, Mickey," said Jillo.

"Oh – sorry. I was thinking."

"What about?"

"Well – Titch says we cracked the secret, right? But there's part of it we didn't crack. What about the babies? The crying? We thought we'd found the answer when we found out about the cassette those guys'd been playing, but we hadn't. So why do babies cry in Weeping Wood?"

"Ah!" Jillo smiled. "I think the excavators found the answer to that one, Mickey."

"How d'you mean?"

"Well – they wrote a report. Dad saw it. It said they discovered the skeletons of seven infants in the foundations of the villa. They'd been buried alive to bring good luck to the place. It was a Roman custom."

"You mean –"

Jillo nodded. "They probably cried for days. It was so horrible that people remembered. Passed it on, like a story. But as years went by, bits of the story got lost or changed. The real babies and the villa itself were forgotten, but people still told one another that babies could sometimes be heard crying in that place, so they called it Weeping Wood. It became a sort of ghost story – a true one."

Mickey gulped. "So we did hear phantoms – those babies really do haunt Sycamore Thicket?"

Jillo smiled. "They did, Mickey, but they might not any more."

"What d'you mean?"

"Well – when the experts have finished examining the bones, they're going to bury them properly, in a churchyard or somewhere. Mum says ghosts usually disappear once that's been done. They're at rest, she says."

Mickey let out a long breath. "Well, I certainly hope so, Jillo." He shook his head. "Poor little things – imagine crying for nearly two thousand years."

Shaz shuddered. "It's the holidays, right? We're supposed to be enjoying ourselves. Let's talk about something cheerful – our new headquarters, for instance."

"Yes!" cried Jillo. "I can see it now – there'll be a shield on the wall with our motto on it."

"We haven't got a motto," laughed Mickey.

"We've got the oath," said Shaz. "We can put that on the shield."

"It'll have to be a big shield," said Mickey. He began reciting the oath, seeing the words written in fancy script on a painted shield, and the others joined in:

"Faithful, fearless, full of fun,
Winter, summer, rain or sun,
One for five and five for one –
THE OUTFIT!"

From somewhere deep in the woods came a single, joyous bark.

⠯ᴵᴾᴾᴼGHOST

Summer Visitors

Emma thinks she's in for a really boring summer,
until she meets the Carstairs family on the beach.
But there's something very *strange* about her
new friends. . .

Carol Barton

Ghostly Music

Beth loves her piano lessons. So why have they
started to make her *ill*. . . ?

Richard Brown

A Patchwork of Ghosts

Who is the evil-looking ghost tormenting Lizzie,
and why does he want to hurt her...?

Angela Bull

The Ghosts who Waited

Everything's changed since Rosy and her family
moved house. Why has everyone suddenly
turned against her. . .?

Dennis Hamley

The Railway Phantoms

Rachel has visions. She dreams of two children
in strange, disintegrating clothes. And it seems
as if they are trying to contact her...

Dennis Hamley

The Haunting of Gull Cottage

Unless Kezzie and James can find what really
happened in Gull Cottage that terrible night
many years ago, the haunting may never stop...
Tessa Krailing

The Hidden Tomb

Can Kate unlock the mystery of the curse
on Middleton Hall, before it destroys the
Mason family...?
Jenny Oldfield

The House at the End of Ferry Road

The house at the end of Ferry Road has just
been built. So it can't be haunted, can it...?
Martin Oliver

Beware! This House is Haunted
This House is Haunted Too!

Jessica doesn't believe in ghosts. So who *is*
writing the strange, spooky messages?
Lance Salway

The Children Next Door

Laura longs to make friends with the children
next door. But they're not quite what they seem. . .
Jean Ure

HIPPO ANIMAL

Have you ever longed for a puppy to love, or a horse of your own? Have you ever wondered what it would be like to make friends with a wild animal? If so, then you're sure to fall in love with these fantastic titles from Hippo Animal!

Thunderfoot
Deborah van der Beek
When Mel finds the enormous, neglected horse Thunderfoot, she doesn't know it will change her life for ever...

Vanilla Fudge
Deborah van der Beek
When Lizzie and Hannah fall in love with the same dog, neither of them will give up without a fight...

A Foxcub Named Freedom
Brenda Jobling
An injured vixen nudges her young son away from her. She can sense danger and cares nothing for herself – only for her son's freedom...

Goose on the Run
Brenda Jobling

It's an unusual pet – an injured Canada goose.
But soon Josh can't imagine being without him.
And the goose won't let *anyone* take him away
from Josh. . .

Pirate the Seal
Brenda Jobling

Ryan's always been lonely – but then he meets
Pirate and at last he has a real friend...

Animal Rescue
Bette Paul

Can Tessa help save the badgers of Delves Wood
from destruction?

Take Six Puppies
Bette Paul

Anna knows she shouldn't get attached to the
six new puppies at the Millington Farm Dog
Sanctuary, but surely it can't hurt to get just a
little bit fond of them...